# SPY DOGS # 1
## A Suspicious Neighbor

Amma Lee

# Introduction

One day as the loveable dog Puggy was spending time with his owner Bill, Puggy noticed something strange happening at the house next door to them. Puggy watched his new neighbor in suspicion as the man carried a large struggling black plastic bag. Being the curious dog that he was, he snuck out of his house and peered into the neighbor's window that night once Bill was sleeping. What Puggy saw shocked him! In that house cages littered the ground and computers were set up everywhere! He saw animals locked up in cages and knew that these animals were the animals that were reported as being kidnapped.

"A Suspicious Neighbor" is a book that takes the reader through the journey of a typical dog and with good fortune on his side, he had achieved a modified technological body that he vowed to use to save the animals and possibly the whole world.

# Chapter One

Puggy wagged his tail in delight as he watched his owner walk onto the front porch. Bill had been gone all day and Puggy had missed him dearly. When Bill made it to the front door, Puggy was already there waiting for him to enter.

"Hey boy," Bill shouted happily as Puggy ran in between his legs. "You must have missed me" Bill said as he got down on his knees and began rubbing Puggy. Puggy barked in delight and licked at Bill's face, causing him to laugh.

"I missed you too" Bill said as he stood up and closed the front door. Puggy tilted his head to the side when he noticed that Bill looked a little different. Even though Puggy was a dog, he was quite perceptive when it came to the well-being of his owner.

Bill made his way to the living room and sat down

heavily on the couch. "I'm okay boy, just a little tired." Bill said as Puggy walked over to him whining. Puggy barked and ran into the kitchen. Puggy watched Bill enough to know that he needed something to drink.

Puggy stood up on his two hind legs and bit at the refrigerator door until he got it opened. When he managed to open it, Puggy took in his mouth a can of cola. He ran back into the living room and handed the can to Bill. Bill laughed in glee.

"You always know what I need. Good boy" Bill said as he took the can from Puggy. Puggy opened his mouth and barked again and sat down wagging his tail happily. He was happy that he was able to help his owner relax a little. Being a human must have been tough because of all of the responsibilities that they had to do. Puggy sat down quietly as he watched Bill drink down his soda. Puggy saw Bill's head began to sway from side to side and a short while later, Bill was fast asleep.

Puggy began to whine a little more because Bill hadn't given him any food before he went to sleep. He scratched at Bill's pants leg, but it was no use. The man was fast asleep. Puggy stood up on all fours and began pacing around the room. He ran into the kitchen to try to see if he could reach the bag Bill always used when it was feeding time.

It was high up and Puggy knew he wasn't going to be able to reach the food. He went back into the living room and barked, but Bill didn't even move a muscle. Puggy walked around in a circle and decided to jump on the couch next to Bill. Finding the remote, Puggy pushed at it with his nose until the television turned on.

"Tonight's story revolves around the disappearance of several local dogs in the past week." Puggy heard the human inside of the television say. He couldn't understand everything that the human said, but he did understand the word "dog." Puggy used his paw to turn up the sound when Bill began making more noises as he slept. "The people in the neighborhood believed that these dogs were kidnapped." Puggy began barking loud as the faces of a few dogs that he'd seen before came onto the television screen. Bill stirred, but remained in his spot.

"Calm down, Puggy" Bill said before his snores could be heard in the room again. Puggy jumped off of the couch and ran to the television screen. He was starting to understand why he hadn't seen these dogs in a while when Bill and he went on their morning walks. Puggy understood the word "kidnapped" as meaning being taken against your will. Puggy sat down in front of the television and whimpered. Puggy needed to find his friends and return them back home.

### 

When Bill woke up, he was shocked to see Puggy in front of the television whimpering.
"Oh, I'm sorry boy, I haven't fed you yet." Bill got up and went into the kitchen. He got the bag of dog food

and begun pouring some food into Puggy's bowl. He sat in front of Bill and wagged his tail, but he was still worried about his friends. He wondered how they were doing and if they were hurt. He wasn't going to let whoever took them get away with their crime.

"Eat up!" Bill said, walking out of the kitchen. Puggy forgot about his worries momentarily and woofed down his food. He was still a little hurt that Bill had forgotten to feed him when he first got home, but he forgave him that time. Bill had been gone all day and even though Puggy was able to get some rest, he knew that Bill hadn't.

When Puggy finished his food, Puggy heard a strange noise coming from outside. He ran to the living room window and poked his head out of the curtain. A new human that just moved on the block the other day was walking towards the house next door with a large black plastic bag. Puggy found the human odd, but could not understand why he thought the human was strange. When Puggy looked at him, he just felt strange. Puggy barked a little when he saw the black plastic bag move around.

"It's too late for that Puggy!" Bill screamed from the other room. Puggy wanted Bill to come in and look at the human before he went into the house. He barked again, but Bill refused to come out. There was something wrong with the human, Puggy didn't dislike the sight of anyone this much unless they were a bad person.

He couldn't get Bill to come in and look though, so Puggy had to investigate on his own. The man looked over at Puggy when he opened the door and Puggy was shocked when the human smiled. It wasn't a smile that Puggy was used to so he immediately felt uneasy. When the man disappeared behind the door, Puggy was still unable to shake his uneasiness. This human was definitely suspicious!

# Chapter Two

When Bill left to go do whatever humans do every day, Puggy watched him drive away out of the window. When Bill was out of sight, Puggy directed his attention to the house next door. It was early in the morning so many of the humans were probably still in bed.

Puggy went into the kitchen and drunk some water that was left in the bowl near his half eaten food from last night and ran outside of the doggy entrance. He shook his body as the chilly air hit his fur; Puggy looked around and saw that nobody was coming so he made his way under the hole in the fence.

Once he was safely in the man's yard, Puggy made his way towards the porch. He brought his head towards the ground and sniffed. After a few seconds he recognized the smell of his friend that the humans called Mannie. Puggy had never seen the small Jack Russell dog come onto this porch before, so the fact that his scent was there did not sit well with Puggy.

He pushed up on his back legs and looked through the window and what he saw surprised him. Puggy saw a lot of screens that he believed is called a "computer." On those screens were weird colors and lettering going across it and it was starting to make Puggy's head hurt.

Puggy had to move over a little bit because he was unable to get a clear view of what was inside of the house. Puggy jumped down and walked over to another window, when he poked his head into the window, he saw the man walking around.

"Where did I put the cage?" Puggy's advanced ears heard the odd human say. "Ah! Here it is" he said as he picked up the cage. The man took a small object out of his pocket and blew into it. The sound that the thing made hurt Puggy's ears and caused him to whimper. Puggy jumped back down on the ground and rubbed his ear with his paws trying to soothe it.

When he jumped back onto the window ledge, he was shocked to see little Mannie walking towards the man. The man quickly grabbed the dog and locked him into the cage. Puggy started barking loud then, trying to get someone's attention.

"My oh my, what do we have here?" the man said as he walked over to the door and opened it. "You are a handsome dog. Do you want to come in and play with your friends?" When the man placed his hand in front of

Puggy's face to get him to smell it, Puggy bit it and ran away.

"Ow!" the man screamed in pain as he ran outside of the house to try and catch Puggy. "Where are you, mangy mutt?" the man said as he searched in the direction that Puggy had ran. Puggy hid beneath some shrubbery where he knew that the human would not be able to find him.

"I got some dog treats for you." The man called out trying to lure Puggy out. Puggy wasn't an ordinary dog that could be fooled easily with treats, sometimes he was, but not this time. The man searched high and low, but eventually gave up and went back inside of the house with a sigh.

Puggy watched the man as he walked back into the house. He waited in his spot for a few more minutes until he was sure that the man wasn't thinking about him anymore. Puggy ran from inside of the bushes and looked into the window again. The man wasn't in the room filled with computers anymore and neither was Mannie.

Puggy didn't remember seeing Mannie on television last night, so he was more than likely taken recently. Mannie was probably the thing that he'd seen moving in the plastic bag last night! Puggy ran back under the fence to get back into the house where he knew he'd be safe. Puggy had to help his friend and the rest of the dogs, but he didn't know how to do it.

Puggy remembered seeing a lot of bottles filled with liquid and he saw a lot of metal objects lying around the house. He didn't know what they did, but he needed to see what it was. It was probably something that would help him save the other animals.

Puggy couldn't try to find a way into the house then because the human was active. He had to wait till it was night time when all the humans slept. He couldn't leave home then also because he didn't know how long he'd be gone. The last time he left the house without permission, when he got home his owner had scolded him and took away his treats for many days. He loved his treats and hated to be scolded, so he'd wait until well after his owner went to sleep.

When Bill came home later that day, he appeared to be more tired than usual. What was even more surprising was the fact that Puggy didn't greet him at the door like he normally did. He had too many things on his mind and he didn't want to forget any details of his plan.

"Puggy! Where are you?" Bill called out, Puggy reluctantly walked out of the bedroom to greet his owner. He barked when Bill bent down to ruffle Puggy's fur. "Are you not feeling well?" Bill asked in concern. "You normally wait for me at the door."

Not wanting to hurt Bill's feelings, Puggy licked him across the face and Bill pushed him away laughing. "Eww never mind." Bill said, wiping Puggy's 'kisses' off of his face. "You must be hungry," Bill said as he went into the kitchen. "I didn't forget this time." As Bill poured the food in Puggy's bowl, he sat there wagging his tail. This time he wasn't wagging his tail because he was happy to eat, but this tail wag was in determination to free his friends.

# Chapter Three

Puggy waited for what appeared to be hours for Bill to fall asleep. When Bill began snoring, Puggy jumped onto the bed a few times to see if Bill would wake up. Puggy barked a few times and when Bill still didn't move an inch, Puggy knew for a fact that he was asleep.

Puggy walked across Bill's exhausted body and licked his face. Bill furrowed his eyebrows and gently pushed Puggy's face away. "I'll play with you later." Bill said as he drifted back to sleep. Puggy had to make this quick because Bill did get up once in a while during the night.

Jumping off of the bed, Puggy gently walked out of the room and once he was a good distance away from the door, he began running down the hall.

Puggy ran all of the way to the front door and to his dismay; there was some type of protective shield covering the way he got out. Puggy began to whine and sat down wagging his tail impatiently. He looked for ways that he could remove the object and he walked up to it and smelled it. It smelled like Bill and this made Puggy believe that he had placed this object on his door.

He bumped his head against it trying to push it aside. Once Puggy got it some distance away from the door, he used his paw to knock it down. He barked in glee once the thing fell down onto the ground exposing his way out. He looked over behind him to make sure that Bill wasn't near him and went outside.

There was no movement outside and Puggy sniffed the air in order to see if there was anyone near him. Once he was sure that he was alone outside, he ran towards the hole in the fence. It was a little difficult for him to get under the fence because his belly was full, but after a few failed attempts to squeeze through, he was finally able to get through it.

He poked his head out of the shrubbery and was met with the pitch black darkness. He didn't see the odd human from earlier so he ran from his hiding spot and ducked under the porch. When he still did not sense anybody, he leapt onto the porch and looked through the window.

Puggy was shocked to see several animals inside of the house running around with devices attached to their bodies. He saw some animals that he recognized and others that he did not know. What were those things that were connected to their bodies? He remembered seeing something similar in that color earlier that day, but it did not look like that. He began whining as he saw the human from before but the human had a different look on his face.

The human's eyes were glowing green, which Puggy knew was not typical for humans. He saw the little dog from across the street again, Mannie, running out of the human's reach whenever the man got close to him. He didn't have those things attached to his body yet and there was a good possibility that he was trying to remain the way that he was.

"Stop running around," The man screamed in anger. Puggy could see the man's face turning red and then all of a sudden the man transformed! Puggy couldn't believe his eyes when the man that he thought was human changed into something grotesque. The once human was pale pink with a big head and a small thin body. Its eyes were bright green and it had a small mouth without a nose.

"Look what you've done," it said. "You've angered my human body to the point of changing me back." Puggy whimpered in fear, he had thought that he could easily rescue his friends when he thought the man was human, but now, he didn't know if he was a match for an alien.

"Taking a human's body is a bit more difficult to get away with. I'll have to leave this place. It's a shame really, I was starting to get used to it." The thing started to chase Mannie again while the other animals stood as still as robots. Even though Puggy was afraid, he had to do something before Mannie was changed into one of those things as well.

Puggy jumped off of the window sill and looked around for an opening to the house. Puggy found an opening to the basement where the glass still littered the ground. He carefully squeezed his body through, making sure not to cut himself on the broken shards.

Once he was fully through, he saw that there were more animals caged up in the basement! Puggy wasn't good with numbers, but he thought that he saw at least thirty animals in cages. The massive room also had many computers. Puggy ran back and forth trying to find how to release the animals.

Puggy bit at the bars trying to pry it open with his teeth, but that only made his mouth sore. He jumped up on top of the computer and pushed some buttons on the keyboard with his nose. Apparently that did something because the cages began to spin around. A few of the dogs began barking in the cages because the motion was scaring them. Puggy pushed at some more buttons and something fell from the ceiling and hit him on the head.

He whimpered in pain, but looked on the floor near the item that fell on him. He had never seen this human word before, "modification," but he picked the cylinder up in his jaws and jumped back onto the keyboard.

After pushing the buttons on the keyboard more, Puggy

was frightened when a loud alarm sounded off in the basement. He could hear the sounds of something running above him and he heard the door slam against the wall.

"Who's down here?" the dog heard the thing's horrible voice. Puggy didn't have anywhere to run so he decided to go into the view of the creature. He barked angrily at the creature. "Ah! The dog from before?" it said, easing its way down the stairs. "It's seems that you wanted to play with your friends after all." It said with a smile spreading across its face. "Give me back the modification and I'll show you how to use it."

Just as the creature said that, Mannie ran in between his legs causing it to fall down the stairs. "Ah!" it cried out in pain as it landed hard on the cement floor. Mannie ran towards Puggy and began licking Puggy's face. Puggy was happy to see his friend as well, but they needed to get out of there quickly. Puggy placed the modification down and barked before picking it up so that he could run away.

"Wait!" the creature screamed, trying its hardest to stand up, but it was too late. Mannie followed closely behind Puggy and in a matter of moments they were out of the house. They ran straight through the hole in the fence and straight into Bill's house. They worked together to push the object back in front of Puggy's door so the creature would not get in. Just as they fully closed the small opening to the house, they could hear the creature calling out to them.

# Chapter Four

Bill jumped out of bed in a hurry when he realized that he was late for work. Puggy normally woke him up when it was almost time for him to wake up, but he didn't this time. "Puggy!" Bill screamed as he ran into the bathroom to brush his teeth.

Puggy was still in front of the door, guarding it with his life, while Mannie slept beside him. Puggy normally would have run to Bill, but he couldn't risk that creature breaking in and hurting Mannie or worse, hurting Bill. After Bill was done in the bathroom, he came out to see what Puggy was doing.

"Didn't you hear me calling Pug? Why didn't you wake me up?" Puggy turned his head in the direction of Mannie and gave a soft bark. "When did this dog get in here? Did you let him in Puggy?"

Bill leaned down in order to grab the tag that Mannie

was wearing. "This is the Richardson's dog." Bill said once he recognized the dog. "They told me that he went missing, but it turns out he was here all this time? I'll give them a call and let them know."

Bill walked away from them then, but Puggy didn't move from his spot. His stomach made the noise it always made when he was hungry, but he didn't want to leave even for his food. "Yeah, I don't know how he got in the house, but he was with Puggy all along. I'm sorry that you had to worry about him." Puggy heard Bill say as he placed the phone back onto the receiver.

Bill whistled two times and Mannie jumped up shivering. "Hey, your parents are coming to get you. You made them worry about you." Bill said as he rubbed Mannie on his head. Mannie barked in delight and wagged his tail. Mannie was happy to see Puggy and Bill because he had the misfortune of being taken from the people that cared for him. The doorbell rang and Bill walked over to it and opened it.

"Thank God he's here." The woman that cared for Mannie said. "I feared the worse. I feared that he was taken just as the neighborhood's animals were."

"Yeah, it's not safe no more for animals. I think Puggy feels the same way because he was sitting by the door like he was watching it when I found him this morning." Bill looked at his clock again and gasped. He picked up Mannie and pushed him into the woman's arms. "I'm so sorry, I don't mean to rush you but I really need to be heading to work." The woman shook her head in understanding.

"Please do forgive me for holding you up. Thank you for calling me and thanks to you too, Puggy." the woman said giving Puggy a huge smile. Puggy barked and allowed his tongue to hang out of his mouth. Puggy was happy that he was able to rescue his friend Mannie, but he had to save the other animals as well. Puggy also needed to see what that "modification" thing did and what was its connection to the animals. Bill went into the kitchen right quick to pour some food into Puggy's bowl.

"I poured in a little bit more food for you for being a good dog." Bill rubbed Puggy on the head and was out of the door.

Puggy ran to the side of the couch once Bill disappeared around the block and pulled out the modification thing. Puggy smelled it and whined when the scent was the same as the creature. He saw a button on the side of it and pushed it with his nose; all of a sudden the "modification" opened up wide and wrapped itself around Puggy's body. Puggy whined loudly and struggled to free himself. After struggling for a while, he froze when he heard someone chuckling.

"It seems as if you're stuck" the pink creature from before said as he opened the living room door. It had some sort of tool in its hands that resembled a key. Puggy barked out in frustration and the creature laughed again. "The object that has wrapped itself around your body is a device that my species uses to control people." Puggy began wiggling his body again. "It's no use" the creature said as it walked towards him. "The objects that the humans use to hold you in place may be easy to break, but alien tools are much more difficult to break!"

The creature laughed and pulled a remote from out of its slimy skin. "You'll be mine!" it said menacingly and pushed the button. When nothing happened, it brought the object closer to its face. "Why is this not working now? I should have control over this animal." The creature kept pushing the button, but all that it did was cause the metal object to expand over Puggy's body. Puggy began howling as the metal object molded all over his body and then absorbed into his skin. Puggy could feel the now liquid spilling all over the insides of his body.

"This is interesting" the creature said standing in front of Puggy's twitching body. "It'll appear the modification works differently on your body." The creature looked at Puggy in confusion. "I'd have to have my alien brother experiment on you because this is out of my knowledge." Puggy could feel his body transforming and he was able to understand what the creature was saying to him. This alien was planning on kidnapping Puggy as well! Once the pain had eased on Puggy's body, Puggy jumped up.

"Do you think that you're a match for me?" the creature said smiling. Puggy had to look up at the creature and he began trying to think of ways to make their levels the same. Just as he thought he wanted to be eye to eye with the alien, two metal poles protruded from Puggy's body.

Puggy was shocked to see the items come from his body since it never happened to him before. He knew that being able to do this was not normal. The metal poles started to spin around in a fast clockwise rotation and before Puggy knew it, his legs were off of the ground and he was coming closer to the alien's face.

"Im…impossible!" the alien screamed once he saw that Puggy had the ability to fly. "The modification shouldn't have given you this ability! Why is it reacting this way with you?" the alien started to push on the button again in order to control Puggy, but none of its efforts worked.

Puggy's intelligence increased and it was as if his body was a machine and if he inputted enough information into it, he'd be able to do more things. Puggy began thinking of ways that he could defend himself from this alien and out of nowhere another metal pole came out of his head.

Puggy saw the alien's eyes widen in fear just as the top of the pole began to change bright red. The alien jumped out of the way just as a red and very hot beam flew past its head.

"A laser beam?!" the alien dropped the key that it was holding and pulled another object out of his pocket. Puggy requested that the laser fire again and just when it had, the alien pushed the button and vanished into thin air! Puggy dropped back onto the floor once the threat was gone and hurried to close the front door. He wasn't able to turn the knob, but he began thinking that he needed fingers to lock the door.

The metal pole that was on his head transformed to a hand! Moving closer, the hand reached out and locked the door. Puggy couldn't believe what had just happened and he was a little afraid that he was able to do these things. His intelligence had increased greatly to the point that he could interpret anything humans said to him. He wondered where the alien had gone and just as he thought this another thought came into his mind. He had to rescue the rest of the dogs next door!

# Chapter Five

When Bill arrived back home later that evening, Puggy was standing on top of the table in the living room looking over to the house next door. He needed to get back into the house again that night so that he could help the other dogs with his new abilities.

"Puggy? How did you get on the table?" Bill asked as he rounded the table to put Puggy back on the ground. When Bill reached him, Puggy barked in a way that Bill had never heard before. Bill jumped back, "What is up with you lately? It's seems like you're a brand new dog."

Puggy looked back at Bill and whined. He didn't mean to bark at Bill that way; he was just going through so much lately that he didn't know how to behave. Puggy walked across the table to Bill, Bill picked up Puggy and put him back on the floor.

"You haven't had a bath so no feet on the table!" Puggy barked and wagged his tail. Bill patted him and Puggy licked Bill's hands, his way of telling him that he's sorry. "I'll get you something to eat."

Bill took the bag from on top of the refrigerator, Puggy was able to figure out that the refrigerator is where Bill stored his food, and he began pouring some into Puggy's bowl. Puggy had been watching the house next door all day and he didn't realize how hungry he was.

"Eat up boy." Puggy ran over to the food and ate it quickly. Puggy would definitely need the food for his adventure that night. When he was done eating, Bill began cooking himself something to eat.

Puggy and Bill watched TV together after Bill was done eating. Puggy was restless as Bill changed the channels. Puggy really wanted Bill to go to sleep so that he could leave without Bill getting upset or monitoring where he was going. Bill stayed up a little longer that night and Puggy began to realize why.

Puggy understood that Bill left every day to go to work and the reason why Bill wasn't going straight to bed was probably because there was no work for him to do the next day. Puggy thought long and hard and came to the conclusion that sometimes work wasn't expected of a human because they needed a break from work. Puggy would have to sit up with Bill until he finally got tired.

Puggy must have waited a long time for Bill to go to

sleep that he must have fallen asleep himself! When Puggy opened his eyes again the house was pitch black. Puggy must have been exhausted because he hadn't slept the night before because of him watching over Mannie all night. Puggy stretched and shook his fur and jumped off of the couch.

He didn't want Bill to hear him walking around so he thought about flying. Just as before, two metal poles shot out of his body and began spinning. The force of the spins were powerful enough to lift him off of the floor. He flew into Bill's room and watched him for a few moments. Bill snored rather loudly so Puggy knew that he wouldn't wake up anytime soon.

Puggy flew quickly down the hall and lowered his body onto the floor. Wishing that he had hands, hands formed from the metal poles and he was able to move the barricade that attempted to keep him inside of the house. He ran quickly out of the house to the neighbor's, the alien's, house. The modifications done to his DNA caused Puggy to move quickly without being detected.

He was on the porch and looking inside of the window in a matter of a few seconds. He was shocked at what he found. Everything was gone! All of the computers and the metal objects that must have been modifications the aliens were using to control the animals were all gone. Puggy decided to create hands again and walked over to the front door. It was open!

Puggy searched the first floor of the house and found no

signs that the alien was ever there. He must have fled when Puggy was asleep. Puggy whined and sat down on the floor. He was too late to save the other animals and that made him sad. Just as Puggy was about to begin whimpering, he thought about going into the basement. With lightning speed, Puggy was in the middle of the basement floor. He found no signs of life, but he did find one computer downstairs that appeared to be broken.

Puggy thought about making a chair so that he could sit in it so that he could try to fix the computer and his metal poles produced hands again. The hands extended in each direction grabbing material to make a chair out of it. Once his hands were satisfied with the loot, they began building. The finished product was a capable chair that could seat people up to five hundred pounds!

Jumping on the seat, Puggy used the hands to type away at some keys. The screen remained black and the speed of his hands began inputting numbers that his brain could not keep up with. After several minutes, Puggy had the computer up and running again. He barked in glee and one of the hands rubbed Puggy on the head.

The computer began updating and uploading information onto the screen. The hands ceased their movements and Puggy read quickly as sentences began coming up on the computer. What Puggy read disturbed him dearly. The aliens were trying to use the animals to overrun the world!

Puggy learned all kinds of information. The thing that

was absorbed into his body was something that was used to modify animals and humans' DNA to make their body run more like a machine and a computer. These devices were also used to control people and animals, but it was supposed to fit onto someone's body like armor, so Puggy did not understand why his was absorbed into him.

He also didn't understand why the controlling device didn't work on him. Puggy also came across some pictures of familiar humans. Apparently the aliens were stealing human's bodies in order for them to blend in well with the community. What alarmed Puggy the most was that their next victim was going to be Bill! He couldn't let that horrible creature take Bill.

Puggy decided to use this house as his base from now on. Puggy had to find where that alien went so that he could get more information on him. He had to study the aliens so that he could understand them better so that he could come up with a plan to stop them from taking animals. Stop them from completing their plans to take over the world. Most importantly, Puggy needed to stop them from hurting Bill. For this to work though, Puggy needed to become a spy.

# Chapter Six

Puggy arrived back at the house later than he intended. He spent the remainder of the night and early morning reading all of the information that the alien had stored in the computer. When he arrived back home, Bill was furious.

"Where have you been?" yelled Bill in anger. "I've been worried sick about you. I thought someone had taken you!" Bill picked Puggy up into his arms and Puggy began whimpering in shame. "Bad dog, how did you even get the piece off of the doggy door?" Puggy lowered his face trying to avoid eye contact. "You're getting locked up in your cage at night until you've learned your lesson."

Puggy's ears shot up and he began barking, his way of protesting. "Don't try to back talk me." Bill said as he carried Puggy into the back room where his cage was being stored. "You will be punished now as well; don't think it's just at night." Bill placed Puggy into the cage and locked it.

"You're staying in time out for ten minutes!" Bill said as he walked out of the room. "You'll get your food once time out is over." Puggy whimpered and bumped his head into the cage doors, but it was no use, the cage wouldn't bulge. Why couldn't Bill understand that Puggy was trying to save him and the world?

The aliens were trying to rule the world with the help of the animals and Puggy was the only one who could stop them! Puggy barked louder, trying to gain Bill's attention again, but either Bill didn't hear him or he just didn't want to come see what Puggy wanted.

Puggy knew that he could easily get out of the cage, but he didn't want to expose his power to Bill. Puggy did the only thing that he could do in that situation, he sat there for those long ten minutes.

"I see you've quieted down" Bill said as he came back to the room. Puggy was lying flat on his stomach in misery. Puggy hated getting time out and he really hated it now because he had so many things to take care of. "You've learned your lesson now, it's time to eat!" Bill opened the door and Puggy shot out of the cage. He shook his fur and stretched, being in that cage was incredibly uncomfortable.

"Are you going to be a good boy for the rest of the day?" Puggy barked and wagged his tail. He *was* being a good boy, Puggy just had to understand that Bill didn't know that he was doing all of this for the better good. After Puggy licked Bill's extended hand, he ran into the kitchen and began eating his food. He was starving and it was almost as if Puggy didn't have enough food.

When Puggy's bowl was empty, Bill came back into the kitchen. "I have to go to the office for a little while." Bill pointed at Puggy, "Be good and stay in the house." Bill walked over to the door with a screwdriver in his hand and some screws in the other. Bill made sure that Puggy wouldn't leave the house when he was gone. Puggy wasn't worried about not being able to get out though; he had the intelligence and material that he needed to get out.

"See you in a few" Bill said and walked out of the house. Puggy ran to the couch and watched in anticipation as Bill pulled out of the drive way and rounded the corner. Puggy ran back to the door and summoned his "hands." One of his hands transformed into a screwdriver and he began unscrewing the screws. Once he had successfully unscrewed the screws, Puggy was out of the house faster than a wild cheetah running after its prey!

Puggy's mechanical hands typed quickly on the keyboard as he sat in his chair trying to figure out where the other alien lifeforms were hiding. He was researching for a while when someone made contact with him over the computer!

A chat box appeared on the corner of the screen and Puggy clicked on it. "Have you acquired any more dogs? Are you able to control them as well?" Puggy was surprised. This alien had to be the creature the alien who was trying to kidnap Puggy was talking about before.

Puggy thought about how to respond to that, but his hands apparently had a mind of their own. "The humans don't suspect a thing as expected. The modification worked as planned and I will send another dog to you for your review."

Puggy was impressed with his own modification; he wouldn't have thought to respond to the creature like that. "Are you still in the same location? I can send the dog to you tonight." Puggy tried to get as much information as he could in order to find out where the kidnapped animals were being held.

"Just one dog? I had to relocate because unfortunately the body that I had met its limit. I am at the blue house on Mayberry Street. Don't send the dog tonight though; I am losing control of a few of the dogs that you've sent me. I will try to fix their controls tonight and won't be able to handle another dog."

Bingo! Puggy had hit the jackpot; he knew where all the dogs were located. He had to spy on the alien for a few hours so that he could learn the Alien's routine, but he knew that he would be able to free the animals tonight!

"Puggy? What are you doing down here? What is that on

your body?" Puggy spun around quickly at the sound of Bill's voice. He had been found out! "A neighbor told me that they saw you come in the house, but I couldn't believe it." Bill said walking over to Puggy with wide eyes.

"Where did those hands come from? How are they coming out of your body? How are you able to use a computer?!" Bill overwhelmed Puggy with questions. Puggy couldn't believe that he hadn't heard Bill come into the house, he had to do something quick. Puggy jumped out of the chair and walked closer to Bill.

"What are you?!" Bill yelled in horror. "What have you done to my dog?!" Bill's voice became loud and Puggy was afraid that he'd draw the attention of other people. Puggy had no choice; Puggy's hand transformed into a spray can with an unknown substance. "What are you doing?" Bill asked Puggy again. Puggy closed his eyes and sprayed the mist into Bill's face. In a matter of a few seconds, Bill was fast asleep.

# Chapter Seven

Puggy sprayed something onto Bill that would make him sleep and make him forget the past hour. Puggy didn't want to do that, but Bill had left him no choice. Puggy didn't want Bill to be harmed and in order to help Bill; Bill had to know nothing about what was going on.

Puggy ran to the broken window in the basement and noticed that it was dark. Puggy had to do this tonight because he didn't want to have to run around and be secretive from Bill. Puggy's metal poles changed back into hands and they cradled Bill in its arms. Running as fast as he could to avoid any type of attention, Puggy made it safely back to his house with Bill.

After placing Bill gently onto the bed and tucking him in, he stared at him. He'd save the animals that the aliens kidnapped in order to save Bill from being a prisoner in the world the aliens wanted to create. Puggy knew that as long as he thought positive, his new body wouldn't fail him. Puggy flew quickly out of the house before his emotions overtook him.

Puggy found the blue house on Mayberry Street with ease and he lowered his body into the bushes so that he'd be shielded from the lights. The house was pitch-black just like the one that he'd been using as his secret base. He scanned the area for a few more minutes before he approached the porch. This time without looking through the window on the porch, Puggy decided to look through the windows under the porch. The basement was filled with many computers and cages with animals trapped inside of them!

Puggy saw the alien typing something onto the computer and it was just as horrible as the last one. Instead of being pink though, the creature was a dark bluish black color. Puggy knew that these aliens were pretty intelligent because they could turn from gruesome monsters into average humans. Puggy had to be more careful with this alien; it didn't seem as sloppy like the other one was.

Puggy watched the alien for hours until he finally picked up its pattern. The alien would leave the computer and go upstairs for ten minutes and come back down and let one of the animals out. The alien would start saying commands to it and wait to see if the animal followed its instructions.

It would do it for all of the animals, which took about an hour and then it would write something down in its notepad. The alien would type something into the computer and go back upstairs. If Puggy wanted to let the animals out, he'd have to do it during the ten minutes it was gone!

The alien had finished typing something into the computer and went upstairs. This was Puggy's chance! Puggy used his laser to cut a big enough hole into the glass and squeezed his body through. The animals looked in his direction as his body hit the floor. Some of the animals wagged their tails in glee and the other ones stood in their cages in silence. These had to be the animals that were still under the alien's control.

Puggy went to the computer and typed 8232 into it which released the locks on the cages. The animals ran out happily and circled Puggy. Puggy's hands typed something into the small computer that controlled the animal's minds and bodies and the animals that were still under control came back to their senses.

"Meow!" The animals turned around as a cat walked across the top of the stairs.
"Intruder" a voice sounded from above and Puggy heard the sound of running coming down the stairs. "Good girl," the blue alien said as he rubbed the cat's head. The cat purred enjoying the affection. "You must be the dog my brother has told me about."

The alien said as he walked over to Puggy and the rest of the animals. "Get back into your cages!" The alien screamed pushing a button on the control pad that it had.

The dogs howled as their bodies forced themselves backwards towards the cage. Puggy stood his ground and barked in a commanding tone, but the dogs continued to walk back until  they were back in their cages.

"Ha! Did you really think that these animals would listen to you? Your little intelligence is no match for mine!" Puggy began growling when the alien stood in front of him. "But your modifications are working differently than theirs." The alien said in an evil voice. "I guess I have to rip yours out so that I can study it!"

The alien quickly produced a whip and tried to hit Puggy with it. Puggy jumped back and his metal poles changed from hands into claws as he pounced on the alien. "Oof!" the alien made a sound of distress when Puggy landed hard on top of him. The alien was intelligent indeed, but it had no strength. Puggy's claws tried to pry the controlling device out of the alien's hands, but the alien whistled as loud as he could, hurting Puggy's and the other animals' ears.

"No matter how much your body advances with my technology inside of you, you're still just a dog!" the alien laughed as he got back up onto his feet. Puggy was in a corner rubbing his sore ears when the alien was in front of him. "Now you're mine!" the alien said as he bent down to grab Puggy.

Puggy was quicker though. Puggy's hands pushed the alien as hard as it could which caused the alien to land inside of one of the open cages. The alien dropped his device and it slid over towards the cat. The cat hissed, but remained in its place. Unlike the other animals, the cat was a typical cat. Puggy's hands closed the cage and inputted the code into the computer which locked the cage.

"Curse you... you mutt!! Let me out this instant!" the alien said trying to break out of the cage. Puggy barked and ran back to the main computer. The alien must have changed the code because he couldn't open the cages to set the animals free! Puggy looked out the window and noticed that morning had arrived; he had to get back home. Puggy decided to take as much information that he could from the computer that the alien was typing into.

"That is sensitive information! Don't touch it!" Puggy transmitted all of the data that the alien had stored on humans, the animals and the aliens themselves into his computerized body. After acquiring all of the information that he needed, Puggy ran towards the window, sad that he had to wait to save the animals. Before Puggy exited through the window, Puggy looked back and saw the cat glaring and hissing at him. Puggy barked and was out of the window.

Puggy ran into the living room after Bill had called his name, "Puggy! I am so sorry that I overslept, I'll get you your food now." Puggy watched Bill shuffle around the when trying to fix Puggy something to eat. Puggy was happy that the spray had effectively caused Bill to sleep for a longer time and erased his memory of yesterday. Puggy wagged his tail as he saw Bill mumbling something about forgetting something important. Puggy's mind went back to the animals. He'd save them for sure because he hadn't failed; he just had to revise his plan. With the new information he acquired last night, he'll definitely save them next time.

Puggy was just happy that the alien, though still with the animals, would be unable to harm them. He was happy that the suspicious neighbor, who turned out to be an alien, had left as well. Puggy would eventually have to locate the missing alien however. He was happy that Bill wouldn't have to suffer from the paws of the neighborhood's animals. Puggy barked as Bill stroked his head gently. Puggy turned to lick Bill's hand and Bill snatched it away quickly.

"Eww!" Bill said laughing. Puggy wagged his tail quickly and barked in glee. As Puggy chased Bill throughout the house trying to lick him again, Puggy failed to notice the small yellow eyes peering at them from their window.

# Charlie Publishing

## A Note About The Author

Amma Lee was a very imaginative child. Starting with picture books at the age of five, she always loved to read and spent countless hours turning the pages of books. She imagined herself in every picture and made up new stories for every book.

Through her middle school years, she devoured every book she could find. She read everything from princess stories to adventure stories that were written for boys. She loved them all!

Now that she's an adult she loves writing for children of all ages and she still reads children's books when no one is looking. She has been writing full time for five years and has never been happier.

Feel free to contact at **charliepublishing@gmail.com**

Made in the USA
Lexington, KY
13 April 2017